A JOURNEY TO 2020

YASHASHWI MAHOBE

Contents

ONE
THE FUTURE

"A virus named COVID 19, popularly known as the Corona Virus had come in the ending of the year 2019, and by way of the year 2020, grew to a massive and deadly pandemic killing tens of millions of people all of the world, leading to lockdown, imprisoning people in their own homes, which brought an economic crisis in many countries across the globe." The history teacher told the class.

The World has totally changed now. It's the year 2100. The 22nd century has begun, and the world is no longer as we understand it now. Technology has totally changed the world. Robots have now grown to be a primary part of human's life. People and robots are living happily together.

"But how did they overcome this pandemic, sir?" asked Nova, being curious and excited to know about the Coronavirus pandemic. The teenage boy, was the best student in the class.

"The people started out operating from their homes and slowly the situations started getting better. But the virus banged once more within the mid-2021 and……"

The bell rang and it was time to go to the tech lab for the student's projects on new gadgets and machines.

"Ok students, we will continue the chapter tomorrow." said the teacher.

The students headed to the lab.

Nova and his best friend Sam, are trying to make a TIME MACHINE. After entering the lab, they grabbed the eBook on quantum physics and started persevering with their venture. The students have to finish, take a look at, and check their initiatives through themselves, and then they could present it to the class and the teacher.

Nova and Sam were not only best friends; however, they are neighbours also.

After school, they went home together and decided to continue making their machine after lunch. Jimmy, Nova's younger brother, and a teenager robot, welcomed him and served him lunch.

Even though Jimmy was a robot, he looks like a nine- or ten-year-old boy. He was just like a human being. He also eats food and he has feelings too.

After lunch, Sam came to Nova's house. There was a huge laboratory in his house. They both started working on the project.

TWO
THE FIRST STEP

Nova had a four-dimensional technological lab in his home. Sam and Nova started creating a blueprint for the Time Machine. Sam was an expert in Quantum Physics and Nova had an intense hold over Mechanics. They first decided to make blueprints individually. They both began on their monitors.

Notebooks and even papers were rare at that time. Everything was written, made, and saved in hard drives and other devices. As the population had increased a lot, humans had occupied most of the land on earth. Trees and other plants are grown in buildings called greenhouses and cutting down trees had turned out to be a crime. As making paper was also inflicting deforestation, it had been stopped, and people started storing every document and records digitally.

Nova completed his design first.

"Hey Sam, look at my design." stated Nova.

They examined Nova's design and Sam observed some faults in his design. The same occurred with Sam's design.

Then they both together worked and made a design that was almost perfect according to them. But there was a huge problem.

Sam and Nova concluded that their Machine was ready to travel to the future, as it was able to travel with the speed of light.

"We can visit the future without problems, but travelling to the past is impossible." said Sam.

"There are few methods I think, we have to figure them out."

"Hey Nova, where's Jimmy?"

"He's assisting mom in the kitchen."

"Jimmy is a robot; he has a million times more knowledge than we have. Why don't we take his help to clear up the trouble?"

"That's a great idea, Sam."

Nova called Jimmy to help them complete the design.

"Hello Guys!" Jimmy entered the lab.

"Hello Jimmy. Can help us make the design for our project." asked Sam.

"It's my pleasure to help you. What can I do for you?"

"Can you please tell me that, is there any method we can travel to the past?" asked Nova

"Let me check within the books stored in me." Said Jimmy.

Jimmy checked all of the books and said, "I have found something."

"That's outstanding!" appreciated Nova, "What have you found Jimmy?"

"Travelling to the past is possible through Wormholes." Jimmy told.

"Yeah! that's cool. We can make wormholes. I've studied to make it in the tenth standard." said Sam.

With Jimmy's help, they completed the design, made the machine, and managed to make wormhole portals that could let them travel to the past.

Now it was time to test the Time Machine.

THREE
THE TIME TRAVEL

"First let's test it to the future", suggested Sam.

"Cool! Let's go to the future, Sam."

"I have a suggestion, Nova."

"What's that?"

"I think you should go to the future as if something happens and you do not succeed to come back, somebody needs to be here, in the present, to help you.

"That's a great and thoughtful suggestion, Sam, I'm so grateful for your help.", commended Nova.

"Dinner's ready children.", Nova's mother called them.

"It has been seven hours since you had started working.", Nova's mother told the children while having dinner.

"We didn't even realize how time has passed while working. The project was so interesting that we forgot about the time.", Sam said.

"Yeah! We enjoyed a lot making the machine.", added Nova.

"Well, which machine are you making boys?", asked Mom.

"That's a surprise mom!!", Nova stated excitedly.

"I hope the machine will help me working in the kitchen.", Mom said laughing.

"I am here to help you mom.", Jimmy enthusiastically uttered.

"That's so sweet of you Jimmy.", Mom said smilingly.

They all had dinner and Nova's mother told them to continue their project tomorrow. Sam went to his home and Nova headed to his room to do the homework he had got from school.

The next day, Nova and Sam met in the school.

"I'm so excited for today, Nova"

"Me too, buddy."

The History teacher was absent because of illness. So, the science teacher took the class.

"Hello children, as this period is not mine, I will just tell you some interesting things going around the world related to science."

The children nodded eagerly.

"I guess you all have heard about the company SpaceX."

"Yes sir. It is an American Aerospace Company founded by Elon Musk in 2002.", Nova answered.

"Very good Nova.", the teacher appreciated. "SpaceX manufactures the most advanced spacecrafts in the world. It is the first-ever aerospace company to settle a civilization on Mars. And now, it is sending people outside the solar system to a habitable exoplanet. SpaceX has announced to initiate this mission at the occasion of their hundredth anniversary, on May 6th, 2102, and has estimated to complete the mission by 2105. And soon, Exoplanets will also be a place of tourism where we all can go."

Students were amazed and were so excited to travel outside the solar system.

After school, Nova and Sam went home together, as they always go, had lunch, and assembled in Nova's lab with Jimmy.

"Nova, in which year you want to go to?", asked Sam.

"Ummmm... I think I ought to go to 2110."

"Oh great! So, let's make it to the future."

"If you stuck anywhere, I'll be there to help you, Nova. I will also go with you.", told Jimmy.

"That's great, Jimmy. Let's go together"

Nova and Jimmy sat inside the time machine.

"As per the calculations, it will take seven and a half minutes to come back, but you can take as much time as you want and after you get into the machine again and press the start button, it'll bring you back exactly after seven and a half minutes from here.", explained Sam.

"That's great, I'm eager to travel to the future.", told Jimmy.

"All the best", Sam wished both of them.

The machine started and disappeared with a flash. The light was so bright that Jimmy and Nova were not able to open their eyes. And after few seconds, when the flash stopped. They both opened their eyes, they observed that the place they had reached was looking like their own lab, but a little changed.

They got out of the machine and saw a boy of 27 or 28 coming inside the lab.

"So, you have reached here. Welcome Nova and Jimmy", the boy said.

"Hey! How do you know us?" asked Nova.

"I am you, Nova, 10 years older. Welcome to the year 2110." The boy said.

"Wow!! Jimmy, we have made it. We have reached the future.", Nova shouted.

They went out from the lab and opened the hologram of the newspaper. They noticed the date. The date showing was April 15th, 2110, exactly ten years from the date they had begun. The headlines of the newspaper stated: "Greatest achievement in human history. After settling a civilization in Kepler-452b in 2106, SpaceX has found the existence of living creatures in titan, one of the moons of Saturn."

Another boy came inside the home shouting, "Oh wow, they've reached here."

It was Sam, ten years older. "Welcome to the future, boys.", he greeted them.

They both went out with elder Nova and Sam. SpaceX and Tesla collectively had opened a tourism system to the Exoplanets. They visited Kepler-425b and stayed there for two days. It is a planet similar to the Earth, but 1402 light-years away from earth.

After coming back, Nova and Jimmy decided to return. They both went to the lab, sat inside the machine, the elder Nova and Sam bade them see off, and Nova tapped on the START button.

Her, Sam was sitting in the lab, counting the time. 7 minutes were over. After some time,

"twenty-seven, twenty-eight, twenty-nine, and thirty."

All of a sudden, a bright light covered the lab and the next moment, the time machine appeared. Nova and Jimmy came out of the machine and narrated Sam their journey to the future.

"That was an amazing journey, Nova."

"They also told me that after visiting the past. You, me and Jimmy will once more travel to them."

"It means our machine will be successful in travelling to the past", Sam stated.

"Yes, it will, I guess", Nova said. "But we are so tired today. We will take a look at the machine for the past tomorrow."

"OK. I also have to complete today's work given in the school. See you tomorrow."

Sam said goodbye to Nova and Jimmy and went to his home.

FOUR

TRAVELLING TO THE PAST

The next day, the history teacher was absent again. This time, the computer teacher arrived to take the period. The students wished him a good morning.

"Hello students. We will study the chapter in the computer period, now let me introduce a new device that is being launched recently."

"Is that the Virtual Reality World Application Resource?", Chris asked.

Chris was the only boy in the class who always was always updated about the new games, applications, and software.

"Right Derek. Virtual Reality World Application Resource, in short, VR-WAR, is a new application that is being launched this Friday. This application, as its name says, is a virtual world. This application or game is generally made for people who want to be alone. They can live in a virtual world where they will be taught to be cooperative with other people by doing enjoyable tasks and games, which require teamwork. And I have got this great opportunity to be one of the team members to create the application.", explained the teacher.

"Wow sir, I'll surely try this application." Nova said.

"But Nova, you are an extrovert, I guess."

"Yes sir, I'll coordinate with people in the application and teach them teamwork, cooperation, and coordination."

"That's great, Nova."

"Sir, will there be any in-game characters in the application?" Chris asked.

"No Chris, every person who wants to play this game will be given a unique character and the judges of the events and tasks, and the trainers of the teams will be recruited by the gaming company, and the trainers will be rewarded as per the performance of their teams.", the teacher answered.

"Will the teams also be rewarded?"

"Yes, the teams will compete in different events and the winning three teams will be rewarded in every event."

"That's great. The people will learn teamwork as well they will be rewarded if they perform well.", Nova stated.

The bell rang and the period was over.

"Ok children, that's all for now. There's homework for you all. If there's any feature you want, to be added, to the application, tell me by tomorrow. If I find it useful and joyful, it will surely be added to the application and you will be credited for that."

The students thanked him and the teacher went out of the class.

After school Nova and Sam had lunch and assembled again in Nova's lab with Jimmy.

"So, Sir Nova, are you ready to travel to the past?"

"Sure, great scientist Sam.", Nova said laughingly. "But I have a doubt."

"What's that, Nova?"

"What if the mouth of the wormhole, we will pass through, gets closed. As we have read that the gravity keeps pushing the walls of the mouth till it is closed."

"That will not be an issue Nova, because while making the wormholes, I have filled the mouths of the wormholes with liquid exotic matter."

"What is that, Sam?"

"Exotic matter is the region or states of matter that have exotic physical properties. It violates the known laws of physics. It has negative mass and hence negative energy which opposes or repels the gravitational push on the walls of wormholes, keeping them open."

"That's so cool, I didn't know that there are particles and matter in the universe which have negative mass and energy. You are a true genius in quantum physics, Sam."

"I have to learn a lot more Nova. So, in which year would you wish to travel?"

"Sam, do you remember the pandemic, our history teacher was telling us about?"

"Yeah, I remember. That was the corona pandemic of the year 2020, right?"

"Yes. I want to know and experience what had happened during the pandemic and how did the world tackle with it."

"So, you want to travel to the year 2020?"

"Yes, Sam."

"Let me set the machine for your journey to the past."

"I'm so excited to go with you, Nova.", Jimmy leapt enthusiastically.

"I'm so eager to see and experience the things and incidents which I have only read in my history book.", told Nova.

"The machine is ready", uttered Sam delightedly.

They sat in the machine, Sam saw them off and Jimmy tapped on to the start button. Once again, a bright light covered the surrounding area and with a flash, the time machine disappeared from the lab.

While travelling through the wormhole, Nova and Jimmy noticed something uncommon in the machine. It took about a minute and again a flash appeared and the next moment the machine was on an empty ground.

They came out of the machine.

"Jimmy, make the machine smaller and put it in your bag, as this place is open and not safe for the machine.", Nova said.

Jimmy did the same and they started looking for somebody who could confirm if they had reached the right place.

After walking a little distance, they noticed a person coming out of a house. They walked to him and casually communicated with him.

"Excuse me, can you please tell us today's date?"

"Yeah sure, it's 30th January, 2020."

They thanked him as they were blissfully satisfied, that they had reached the time they wanted.

There was a public library nearby. They went into the library and grabbed a newspaper. They were astonished to see a number of books, magazines and newspapers made up of paper.

They checked the date again, it was January 30th, 2020. The newspaper stated that the first case of COVID-19 or the coronavirus had been found in Washington DC.

Setting the machine for the return journey they put it in the bag, deciding if anything unfamiliar happens unexpectedly, they would be able to use the machine immediately, to return to the future. This was Nova's suggestion.

"That's a great idea, Nova", said Jimmy.

They left the library and found an empty place to bring the machine out.

Jimmy entered the machine to set it to go to the future, but after a few seconds, he shouted. Nova rushed there and asked Jimmy, "What happened?"

Jimmy uttered worriedly, "Nova, the machine is not working."

FIVE

STARTING A NEW JOURNEY

After knowing that the time machine is not working, Nova and Jimmy got panicked for a while, then Nova got an idea. He checked the machine and closely looked into the wirings of the machine.

"I have checked the wirings and I don't think there's any fault in it, there can be a problem with the wormholes and the quantum calculation. As I am a little poor in quantum physics and quantum mechanics, I would need a book for the subjects' proper information. Jimmy, can you please check for the books in your memory."

Jimmy checked for the books in his memory and storage, and informed Jimmy.

"I remember that I had the books in my memory, but I don't find them now. I don't know how they have been deleted."

"Can it be, due to travelling through the wormholes?"

"Yes, I also think that to be the reason. I was feeling a bit awkward while travelling through it."

"I was feeling weird too. I had a headache after coming out of the wormhole."

"What can we do now, Nova?"

"As it's getting dark, let us find a shelter first and take some rest. My head is aching badly. We'll take rest today and after that, we'll look out for a solution for this trouble."

They saw a white house with a blue roof at some distance. It was a beautiful double-storeyed house. They went there and knocked at the door to ask for shelter. A man came out. He was Japanese, aging around thirty-five.

"Hello uncle, my name is Nova and he is my younger brother Jimmy."

"Hello, I'm Mr. Haruto. How can I help you, children?"

"Can we please get some place for a few days?"

"Yes, you can live here."

There were only two people living in the house, Mr. Haruto and his wife Mrs. Hatsumi. They both were very kind and helpful. They treated Nova and Jimmy as their own family members. They all had dinner together. Jimmy had tasted Japanese food for the first time.

"So delicious. I've never eaten this before.", Jimmy screamed.

"Thank you for having us. We loved the dinner.", Nova said.

"That's so sweet of you children. I am glad you liked the dinner.", Mrs. Hatsumi said smilingly.

After the dinner, Mr. Haruto showed them a room where they could take rest. The room was very beautiful and well organised.

Jimmy and Nova were so tired that they fell asleep immediately.

Mr. Haruto and Mrs. Hatsumi did not have any children so, they were quite happy to have Nova and Jimmy with them.

The next day, they started working on the machine. After a while, they decided to go out in search of books related to quantum physics in the nearby library.

"Nova, let's look around the city first.", Jimmy suggested.

Nova agreed. And they visited many famous places across the city.

"That's the Statue of Liberty. I have seen it's pictures in a book I have. It is about the famous sculptures and monuments during the twentieth and twenty-first century", Jimmy said to Nova, pointing towards the Statue.

"Yeah. I have also seen it. This statue is so beautiful, but it will be damaged in World War III.", Nova stated.

They visited a number of other tourist places across the city, like the Brooklyn Bridge, The Museum of Modern Arts, The Empire State Building, and so on.

They were quite excited to visit and see those places, they had only read in the books. After the trip they went to the library and got some books issued related to quantum science, and went home.

Mr. Haruto had just arrived from the office. He was working in an IT company at some distance from his home.

"Welcome home, children. The water is ready for you. Have a bath, and then we will have dinner.", Mrs. Hatsumi said.

They had dinner together.

"Uncle, can we stay here as paying guests?", Nova asked.

"You both are like our own children. You can stay here as long as you want.", said Mr. Haruto.

"But you don't even know us very well."

"You children are so kind and helping. Jimmy also helps Mrs. Hatsumi in her household works. And because of your noble behaviour, I trust you."

"Thank you so much, uncle. We are so grateful to you."

Nova went to his room where Jimmy was reading the book they had got issued from the library.

"I found some information about the wormholes, but I don't know how to find or how to make one.", Jimmy told Nova.

Nova was still thinking about Mr. Haruto. He did not want himself and Jimmy to be a burden for him.

"Jimmy, I don't want that I and you should be a burden to Mr. Mr. Haruto. So, I have thought that I will find a job. We will live here as paying guests."

"That's a great idea, Nova."

The next morning, Nova went out to find a job for himself. Finding a job for a boy of seventeen would be a difficult work, but as Nova was fairly good at mechanics and had a lot of knowledge as compared to the people of that time, he got a job as an engineer in a company.

He went home and told the family about his new job. They were so happy, but Mr. Haruto still did not want to be paid by them.

"You do not have to pay us to live here. You are like our own children."

"If I am like your own child, it is my responsibility to help the family financially also."

Nova had a strong point. Mr. Haruto agreed and they started living together happily.

About The Next Part

Nova and Jimmy started living happily with Mr. Haruto and Mrs. Hatsumi, but here's when their new life begins. There are a lot of challenges and adventures coming into their life, and also a beautiful story. Let's see how they face the challenges, combat the pandemic and manage to get back home...